THE HAUNTED HOUSE

WRITTEN BY
CAROLYN CLARK
ILLUSTRATED BY
KEITH NEELY

Macmillan McGraw-Hill

New York   Farmington

The old Jones house was the spookiest place in town. No one had lived there for as long as Jim or Adam could remember. Vines covered the yard and most of the house too. Newspapers, delivered long ago, lay in the grass. A broom leaned against the front door, as if someone would come and make the house clean again.

The twins walked by the house twice a day, once on the way to school and once on the way home. Jim always walked by as fast as he could, but Adam always stopped and stared through the rusty iron fence. The house's empty windows, like eyes, stared silently back.

Suddenly one chilly October morning, Adam and Jim heard loud screeching noises coming from inside the house.

"I knew it!" Adam exclaimed when he caught up with Jim. "Old Mr. Jones was a pirate. He hid all his treasure inside the house. That screeching is the giant parrot who guards the treasure."

"Or maybe the ghost of the giant parrot who guards the treasure," shivered Jim. "Let's get out of here! I don't know why you always have to look at that dumb house."

"Oh, come on," said Adam. "You aren't scared, are you? If it is a parrot, it's just a big bird. We'll take it some crackers. They like crackers. While the parrot is busy eating, we can find the treasure. Then we can get a new computer and maybe even new bikes. Come back with me after school tomorrow."

"Adam, you're just making this up!"

"Maybe, but if I have to go by myself, I get ALL the treasure, and the computer, and the—"

"Well—okay, I'll go," Jim said. He really did want a new bike.

The next morning, the boys stuffed their pockets with crackers. Then, after a long after-school soccer practice, they headed back to the house.

"Wait, Adam. Something looks different. Something has changed. This is weird."

"No more noise," Adam hissed. "This is a top secret mission. Don't even let the leaves rustle under your feet."

"Stop telling me what to do if you want quiet," muttered Jim.

Adam and Jim opened the iron gate slowly. They tip-toed and crawled through the scratchy bushes and tan-gled vines to a big window at the side of the house.

"I think we can climb in here," Adam whispered, close to Jim's ear.

"Hope Polly likes crackers, not people," Jim whispered back.

"SSSSHHHHHHHH!"

"SSSSHHHHHHHH! yourself," said his still nervous twin.

They peeked over the windowsill, but they didn't see a parrot.

What they saw was a big, dark shadow on the wall. The shadow of an arm moving up and down, holding a huge hammer.

"Bang, Bang, BANG!" They couldn't see what the hammer was hitting, but whatever it was, it was getting smashed!

"Bang, Bang, BANG!"
"OOWWWWWOOOOOOOOOO!!!!!"
"AAAAAAAAAAHHHHHHHH!!!!!"
Adam and Jim screamed, too, and ran home as fast as they could.

At dinner, Dad said, "I heard some news today. Someone has finally moved into the old Jones place. Her name is Mrs. Grant."

"I'm so glad," Mom said. "I can't wait to meet her."

"Oh, and by the way, boys, what's with all the cracker crumbs on the floor?" Dad asked. "It looks like you've been feeding a giant parrot."

Adam looked at Jim. Jim looked at Adam. They both shrugged. Then they squirmed through the rest of the meal.

Back in their room, Jim shut the door and said, "That was a lady making those noises? What was she doing in there?"

"I don't know about you, but I'm walking on the other side of the street from now on!"

For the rest of the week, Adam and Jim carefully avoided the old Jones house. They crossed the street and hurried by at top speed without looking back.

Saturday morning the boys were helping Mom rake leaves in the front yard, when they saw a woman struggling down the sidewalk with a cart full of groceries.

"Hi!" Mom said. "You have quite a load there. Could you use our help?"

"Thank you," said the woman. "Normally I could manage, but I banged my hand with a hammer the other day, and it's still awfully sore."

"Oh, that must have hurt!" said Mom.

"Yes, I really howled!"

Mom and the woman laughed, and the woman said, "I'm Sarah Grant. I just moved into the old Jones house."

"Uh-oh," Adam whispered to Jim under his breath. "But she doesn't look scary at all! She even looks a little like Mom."

"Come on, boys, let's help Mrs. Grant home with her groceries. Sarah, these are my sons, Jim and Adam."

"I'm glad to meet you. How old are you two? I'd guess about nine."

"Right," the boys said.

"Oh, that's perfect!" said Mrs. Grant. "My son Ricky is nine too. He will be happy to know there are boys his age close by. He and his dad will be moving here as soon as school is out."

"She's nice," Jim whispered. "I think we were wrong."

"Maybe," Adam whispered back. "But they *could* have a parrot."

When they got to the new Grant house, Mrs. Grant said, "Please excuse the mess. I'm fixing up the house, and it is a really messy job. It's a noisy job too. People must wonder what in the world is going on in here!

"Say, Adam and Jim, would you like to play some computer games while your mom and I have a cup of coffee? I have my son's favorite here—it's called 'Scary House.' "

Adam and Jim looked at each other and laughed. "Sure," they said. "We like that game too!"